About the Book

Noko, son of the Indian chief El Quibian, was the first to see the strange sails moving against the far horizon. He had heard stories of white men in great ships. Could they be coming to Veragua?

He hurried to tell his father, who decided to meet the newcomers in friendship. But when the Spaniards discovered gold inland and started a permanent settlement, the Indians knew they must drive away these intruders.

Instead El Quibian and his family were captured and held as hostages. They all managed to escape, however — all but Noko, who was forced to sail with the Spaniards to La Española. Would he ever see his home again? Did he face slavery? Or death?

This exciting adventure story is the first to tell of the voyages of Columbus through the eyes of an Indian boy. A vividly realistic book, based in large part on the diaries of the son of Christopher Columbus.

About the Author and the Artist

WILMA PITCHFORD HAYS has distinguished herself with her numerous books for children, chiefly on historical subjects. Mrs. Hays lives in Venice, Florida, and summers in Orleans, Massachusetts.

Well-known artist PETER BURCHARD has illustrated several of Mrs. Hays' previous books. His strong, vital illustrations add to the action and excitement of this story.

Noko,
Captive of Columbus

by Wilma Pitchford Hays

illustrated by Peter Burchard

Coward-McCann, Inc.   New York

© 1967 by Wilma Pitchford Hays
Library of Congress Catalog Card Number:
AC 67-10415
PRINTED IN THE UNITED STATES OF AMERICA

For David and Stephen

CUBA

La ESPAÑOLA

JAMAICA

Santo Domingo

CARIBBEAN SEA

VERAGUA

SOUTH AMERICA

N

Noko was watching the deep green water for a sea turtle and did not see the wave until it lifted and tossed his dugout. He threw himself forward to steady his tree-trunk canoe. He could swim as well as a fish, but he did not want to lose the turtles he had caught. They would make a feast for everyone in his father's house.

Noko saw that the weather was changing. The swells were higher. The sky was filled with hurrying white clouds and the sun set hot and red. Dolphins playing on the surface of the water suddenly raced away.

Noko pushed back the dark hair which hung straight to his black eyebrows. "Hurakan," he muttered, and began to paddle toward the mouth of the wide river which emptied into the sea.

The tide was low when Noko tried to cross the sandbar which almost closed the mouth of the river. A wave rolled over him and upset his dugout. When the sea drained back, he stood in waist-high water, and his brown skin burned where the coral sand had scratched him.

His dugout lay upside down. The turtles had escaped and were waddling off across the bar. He had to let them go for he needed to rescue his dugout before another wave carried it away.

Noko pulled it onto the high bank of the river and emptied it. When he lifted his head, he saw, far out at sea, a strangely shaped cloud which seemed to ride the water. Beside it another cloud appeared, then another.

Noko had never seen clouds like these, dark patches standing out against a blood-red sky. They were wide at the bottom and came to a point at the top, shaped like tips chipped from stone for a cane spear.

As he watched, the pointed clouds sailed along the water far, far out. Noko was not sure whether he was seeing something real, or something drawn upon the sky by the storm god, Hurakan.

They look like sails, Noko thought, but they are not like the square palm sails of our great canoes. These are not like the sails used by any tribe which comes to trade up and down the coast of Veragua. What men ride in such great canoes?

Whoever they are, *they are not like us.*

Suddenly Noko was afraid, for he remembered something he had heard but never really believed. From time to time, the men from other tribes who came to Veragua told a strange tale. The visitors said that many moons ago men with light skin, who covered their bodies with cloth, had come to the islands off the coast, then sailed away.

These light-skinned men were commanded

by a man called Columbus. Some visitors said Columbus was a man-from-heaven. He had been just and paid the tribes for all he took. Others said his great canoes held thunder-sticks which killed men from a distance, and he would surely destroy the tribes if he came again.

Noko knew his father, El Quibian, would want to know about the strange sails on the sea, for El Quibian ruled the Guaymi people of Veragua who lived along the river. Noko paddled upriver as fast as he could and pulled his dugout onto the bank before his father's open-sided house.

He had scarcely ducked in under the palm-thatched roof when rain beat down upon it

like a drum. His father's wives were serving the evening meal in the center of the large house, which was protected by tall trees growing thick and close about it. Several village children were eating with his brothers and sisters, for it was the custom of his people to share anything they had with anyone who needed or wanted it.

Noko's father was enjoying the baked fish, maize cakes, cassava bread, and fruit from his pineapple fields. Noko's news was not something to be shouted above the din of rain and wind and the laughter of women and children. Besides, he was hungry. He sat down to eat, knowing that his father would go to his hammock behind a palm-leaf curtain in another part of the house when he had eaten. There Noko could talk to him alone.

His father's eyes were closed when Noko came and stood beside him. On a cord around his neck, El Quibian wore a circle of hammered gold. The markings on it showed that he was a *cacique,* or king. Noko wore a similar locket of gold on his brown chest, for he was El Quibian's first son.

"Father," he said, "I must tell you something important."

"Yes?" his father said without opening his eyes.

"Today my dugout overturned on the bar. When I climbed to a high point on the riverbank, I saw strange canoes far at sea."

Now his father opened his eyes. "Caribs?" he asked.

Noko shook his head. Once he had seen the canoes of the man-eating Caribs, who had always been enemies. The men of the village had gone out to fight the Caribs and driven them back to the islands from which they came.

"These canoes must be very big," Noko said, "for their sails are wide and come together like this." He made a tent of his hands and watched his father's face. He could not easily speak of his fear.

"Were the men on these strange canoes like us?" El Quibian asked.

"I saw nothing but dark sails against a red sky," Noko said.

For a long time his father was silent. At last he said, "Hurakan changes the shape of sky and water with his wind. Perhaps you saw waterspouts."

Noko was relieved and a little ashamed that he had made such importance of what might be only waterspouts. He turned to go but his father stopped him.

"Yet you may have seen true," El Quibian said. "For many years the wise men of our tribe have felt that some new and great change is about to take place in our world. All the tribes, up and down our coast, feel this change coming without knowing what it is to be."

Noko waited. It was not often his father talked to him like this.

"They could be the men-who-are-not-like-us," El Quibian added.

"We should go to meet them and drive them away," Noko cried.

"No," El Quibian said. "If they come, we will offer them food, then let the strangers show whether they are friend or enemy."

Noko felt better. His father was a man of good will, but he was strong and courageous and not easily fooled.

Safe in his home sheltered by the jungle, Noko heard the hurricane rage with winds so high that he was sure no ships could remain afloat on the open seas. But when the storm had passed, a runner came to El Quibian saying that strange ships had crossed the bar and anchored in the deep harbor inside the river's mouth. Boats from these ships were on their way upriver now.

El Quibian called for a canoe and paddlers and went to meet the strange men.

"Let me go," Noko begged.

"Not until I know the kind of men they are," his father said.

The boy followed along the bank of the river, hidden by the trees and vines. He watched while his father's canoe drew alongside the boats of the strangers. The river was so wide here that Noko could not hear what they said. He could see men dressed in fine clothes talking to his father, then they turned their boats and parted peacefully.

Noko ran all the way home to meet his father. "Are they good men?" he asked. "Where did they come from? What do they want?"

"They seemed friendly," El Quibian said. "They brought interpreters who know our language, and I spoke with Bartholomew Columbus, the brother of Admiral Christopher Columbus. He said they came from a land called Spain. The Admiral wants us to visit him on his ship tomorrow."

"Can I go this time?" Noko begged.

His father nodded. "Tell the women to get the whole family ready to go," he said. "We will show the strangers that we have no fear of them."

Noko was one of the twenty paddlers who

brought his father's great canoe alongside the Admiral's ship the next afternoon. The Spaniards seemed surprised at the size of the canoe made of one great tree trunk, ten times the length of the tallest man. El Quibian, with his large family of children and the women, sat under a palm-leaf roof, protected from the sun and spray.

Noko managed to follow his father on board the Spanish ship by carrying some of the gifts El Quibian had brought: fruits, cassava bread and maize.

Indian interpreters repeated the Spaniards' thanks. "We are grateful," they said, "for we have little food on the ships and it is very bad."

Noko saw that, hungry as the Spaniards were, they seemed most interested in the lockets of hammered gold which his people wore. Even Admiral Columbus had eyes only for the gold. He lifted the heavy circle around El Quibian's neck and looked into it at his own blurred image.

The Admiral's reddish hair was mixed with gray. His tall body was stooped and his long face lined. His eyes were tired as if he had had little sleep or rest for days. Yet he was as pleased as a boy when El Quibian took the cord from around his neck and gave his gold circle to Columbus.

"Where did you get the gold to make the mirrors?" Columbus asked.

El Quibian pointed toward the far-off rugged mountains. "My men go a long way to collect gold," he said, "and they cannot eat or take their wives with them, for the gold is a gift from the King-of-the-Sky who unearths nuggets with the great rains he sends in season."

Then El Quibian turned to his family and told them to give their circles of gold to the Spaniards as gifts. Noko gave his locket to a boy about his own age with flaming-red curly hair.

"I am Rodrigo and I thank you," the young man said, and he handed Noko a tinkling bell. He laughed when he saw that Noko understood him. "You are surprised? I learned some of your tongue from Indians on our ships."

For many days the Indians and Spaniards lived as friends while the ships lay at anchor in the deep harbor of the river. Bartholomew Columbus, with sixty-eight men and Indian guides, went far upriver and into the mountains in search of gold. The Admiral ordered the remaining Spaniards to build houses near the mouth of the river at the foot of a hill.

Many of the Spanish workers were no older than Noko. He liked to bring his dugout ashore where they camped and watch and listen to them. He was learning a little of their language and sometimes talked with the boy with the flaming-red curls.

Rodrigo sang when he enjoyed what he was doing and sulked when he did not. He was sulking as he tried to thatch the sides of a timber house.

"Here," Noko said, "it is easy." Quickly he wove the palm leaves as he had seen the women do it. "Perhaps you are a better paddler," he teased.

"I'm not a sailor," Rodrigo said. "I volunteered for this voyage for adventure. But now I must build houses while others seek gold. We are not even allowed to leave the camp."

"Why?" Noko asked.

"Admiral Columbus knows that some of the men would go against his orders and trade for gold at the end of a gun," Rodrigo said. "The Indians would be angry and there might be a fight. It has happened with other Indians, but we have always won the skirmishes."

This young Spaniard was very sure of himself, Noko thought, yet he liked Rodrigo. They finished the thatch and the day's work was done.

"If you cannot leave here," Noko said, "we'll fish on the river in front of the camp. The small fish, titi, come close to shore in the rainy season. If we swim among them, they are frightened and leap out of the water. When they fall on the bank, we have only to pick them up."

"I cannot swim," Rodrigo said, frowning, for it did not please him to admit that there was anything he could not do.

"I'll swim," Noko said. "You catch the fish before they flop back into the water."

Their shouts of excitement brought other young men from the camp. They scrambled along the riverbank catching the small silver fish. When they had enough, the boys wrapped each fish in damp leaves as Noko showed them. The fish baked fast. Eating together in the dusk, the young Spaniards talked about the gold they would take home and the things they would buy in the shops of Spain.

Noko listened and grew thoughtful. When he reached home, he said to his father, "The Spaniards have been gone in the mountains a long time. Will they take all our gold?"

Noko did not need gold to buy anything. But his family had given the visitors the gold circles which they had always worn about their necks. They would need more pure nuggets to hammer new necklaces.

El Quibian gave Noko a little smile. "They will take none of our gold," he said. "I told the guides to take the Spaniards to the mountains of Urira."

Noko grinned at his father's cleverness. The men of Urira had often stolen gold from Veragua. By sending the Spaniards to Urira, El Quibian kept his old enemies busy and saved his own gold.

Bartholomew Columbus and his men finally returned, rejoicing. They had traded with the Urira Indians for many circles of gold and for cords of pure twisted gold which the Indians wore around their heads. And they had found nuggets of gold at the foot of trees where the rain had washed away the earth.

At once the Spaniards began to build more

houses. They put up a large storehouse which they filled with goods from the ships. Noko watched them bring ashore a small cannon and casks of gunpowder. Why did the visitors need so many houses and guns in a camp? He spoke of it to Rodrigo, being careful to be polite and not seem anxious for them to leave.

"Now that you have so much gold, you will want to take it home soon?" he asked.

"Now that we've found so much gold, half of us must stay here and settle this country for Spain," Rodrigo said in disgust. "I hope I am not chosen to stay."

Alarmed, Noko went at once to his father and told him what Rodrigo had said.

El Quibian nodded. "I have talked with the *caciques* of neighboring tribes," he said. "It is one thing to entertain visitors, to give food and gold to these men-who-are-not-like-us. It is another thing for these strangers to settle upon our land and plant their flag and call all they see their own."

"What can we do?" Noko asked. "The guns on the ships shoot as far as their camp. We have only spears and arrows."

"We have plans," El Quibian said. "Already men from many tribes are gathering upriver beyond the curve of the headland. Tomorrow night before the moon is up, we will paddle downriver and set fire to the houses the Spaniards have built, then they will return to their ships. Our men will line the riverbank and never let them come ashore again."

His father had scarcely finished speaking when a runner burst into the house. "The Spaniard called Diego Mendez," he said, "went upriver last night and found our warriors' camp. This Mendez had only a handful of paddlers, yet he went ashore alone to face a thousand of our men. Our warriors yelled and threatened him, but no one wanted to be the first to strike a man of such courage. Surely Diego Mendez must be favored by the King-of-the-Sky to be so fearless."

Noko saw that his father was disturbed. By

now all the Spaniards would know of the planned attack. Before his father could speak, another runner arrived.

"The fearless Mendez is approaching in a canoe," he said.

El Quibian turned to Noko. "Go meet the Spaniard," he said. "Tell him not to enter my house and frighten my children and the women. I will come to meet him, and hear what he has to say."

Noko ran to the door, but Mendez and a companion were already before the house. Noko stood in front of them and gave Mendez such a push that he almost knocked him down.

"You are no longer welcome in my father's house," Noko cried.

Then he saw the curly red hair of Mendez's companion. Rodrigo smiled, but Noko had no answering smile for his former friend.

"We have come to talk of peace," Diego Mendez said, as if nothing had happened.

El Quibian appeared, sat down in the doorway to bar the way into his house, and waited without speaking.

Diego Mendez opened a small box he had brought with him. "Admiral Columbus sent you a gift, a barber's kit," he said, "to show that we want to be your friends."

Noko looked at the box in the Spaniard's outstretched hand. He was curious, but he would not show it.

"I have here a small mirror, a comb and a pair of shears," Mendez said. "We will show you how much better these instruments work than the sharpened stones you use to hack off your hair."

He sat down upon the ground. Rodrigo carefully combed the black hair and beard of Diego Mendez. No one said a word while he snipped, snipped with the shears. When he had finished, Mendez's hair was trimmed evenly without a ragged jag.

Noko was impressed. He saw that his father was, too. El Quibian allowed Rodrigo to come forward and comb and trim his hair.

Mendez gave El Quibian the barber's kit.
"It is yours," he said, then added, "we are hungry and have not eaten today."

Noko knew his father would not refuse
food to anyone. When they were inside the
house, Rodrigo said, "Are we friends again?"

This time Noko smiled and sat down beside him.

As they were eating, Diego Mendez noticed
an old arrow wound on El Quibian's arm.
"Tomorrow," he said, "I will bring you med-
icine to heal that."

Late the next afternoon Mendez and Bartholomew Columbus returned with two boats. El Quibian came from his house to meet them. Mendez bent over El Quibian's arm as if to look at his wound, and suddenly seized him. At the same time he shouted, and Spaniards rushed from behind the trees around the house.

They carried off El Quibian and his wives and children. Noko kicked and fought, but he was overpowered and tossed into the boat in which his father was a captive.

El Quibian heard the cries of his wives and children and he spoke to Bartholomew Columbus. "Let us go. I will give you much gold which I have hidden in the woods nearby."

"Gold will do us no good if we are killed," Bartholomew Columbus said. "We must keep you as hostages. As long as we have you, the Indians will not attack our settlement."

El Quibian's hands and feet were bound with rope. "Watch him carefully," Bartholomew Columbus said to the pilot of the boat. "Don't let him escape, for he is an important man."

"You may pluck out the hairs of my head and beard, one by one, if he gets away," the pilot said. He guided the two boats carrying the captives down the river toward the ships.

Noko's ankles were tied together and he was packed in so closely among the weeping women and his smaller half brothers and sisters that he could scarcely move. He could see his father in the bow of the boat.

El Quibian was acting strangely for a brave man. He moaned and dropped his head forward as if he had fainted. When the Spaniards offered him water, he fell against them helplessly, crying that the ropes were too tight.

Either the Spanish pilot took pity on El Quibian or was afraid of injuring his valuable hostage, for he loosened the ropes. He left only a rope about the *cacique's* waist, and he held onto it himself. Noko saw that his father sat quietly now.

It was a long ride downriver to the ships, and the captives bent forward in silence to keep the sun out of their eyes. Noko grew dizzy from the heat and dozed lightly. Suddenly he was awakened by a splash, then cries from the Spaniards. Night had fallen but Noko guessed that his father had jumped overboard. El Quibian had complained earlier just to prepare this way of escape. Would he get away?

The pilot braced himself and held tightly to the rope which was still around the *cacique's* waist, but El Quibian was strong and the pilot let go rather than be pulled into the deep water.

The Spaniards lifted their guns. They could not see the swimmer, but they shot at the sounds he made in the water. Noko shouted and the women and children cried out, too. They made such a racket that no one could hear El Quibian's movements.

When Noko knew that his father had escaped, he bent his head and closed his eyes.

Tears of relief squeezed between his eyelids. Now his father would rally the warriors and rescue his family.

The captives were taken on board one of the ships anchored in the river harbor. One by one, they were forced to drop through a hatch to the hold below. The hatch cover was closed and heavy chains fastened across it.

In the darkness Noko tried to stand up and bumped his head on the beams above. He crouched and tried to think, in spite of the crying of the women and children. Perhaps he could lift the cover of the hatch, for he was strong.

He felt along the beams over his head, moving carefully so he would not step on anyone. His hand came to an empty place. He felt along the edges and realized that the hatch, the only opening out of the hold, was built up higher than the deck, much higher than he could reach.

As he stood, trying to think what to do, he

heard sailors talking together as they stood on guard above. One of them must have leaned against the hatch, for the heavy chains rattled. Noko was filled with despair. There was scarcely a crack to let fresh air in, let alone an opening to crawl through. They could not escape.

Day or night, it was dark in the hold. The captives saw light only when the hatch was uncovered and food handed down to them. Each day Noko tried to cheer his brothers and sisters by saying that their father would surely come and rescue them.

Noko learned to tell when night had come, for then the sailors went to their beds and the ship grew quiet. He could hear the two guards talking together above.

One night Noko overheard the guards say that the Admiral was waiting for a heavy rain to swell the river and raise the water over the bar so his ships could get out of the harbor. Then he planned to leave for the island of La

Española, where he had built a settlement on his first voyage from Spain.

From La Española, Admiral Columbus would send back ships to help the men he was leaving behind in Veragua. The Admiral's brother and Captain Diego Mendez were to remain in charge at the settlement on the riverbank.

Noko realized that his father and the warriors had not burned the settlement houses as they had planned. Had the guns of the Spaniards stopped them? Or was El Quibian unwilling to attack while his family were hostages?

Noko did not believe the Spaniards would keep a promise even if his father offered the safety of the settlement in exchange for his family. Any hour, if a rain came, the ships would move out of the river to the sea. If Noko and his family were to escape, it must be now.

In the hold, Noko found bags of stones and sand which were used as ballast. He told

the women and his brothers and sisters what
he hoped to do.

"When we hear the guards and know it is
night," he said, "we will carry bags of sand
and stones and pile them high under the
hatch. Then I'll moan and cry that I am sick.
When the two guards open the door of the
hatch to see what is the matter, I'll leap up

and pull them down before they know what has happened.

"Be ready to climb on the bags and reach the deck. Wait for no one," he warned. "Run and leap over the rail and swim for shore."

The women and children nodded. They knew the risk they would be taking, but it was better to drown than be carried far from home.

When the bags were piled up, Noko began to cry out as if he were in pain. The children joined him in anguished howls.

The guards only rattled the chains. One shouted, "Quiet down there. How's a man to sleep?" For the guards were not required to keep awake, only to stay on the deck beside the hatch.

"Who can sleep anyway," the other guard growled, "with the deck awash with waves?"

Noko was really troubled now. Waves on the river meant flooding from a heavy rain in the mountains. By morning the water would rise and the ships could get over the bar to sea. Yet no matter how much he moaned and called, the guards would not open the hatch.

The children began to cry. What could Noko say to them now that his plan had failed? Then he heard another voice above, a voice he knew.

Rodrigo was saying to the guards, "Why do you sleep on this wet deck? You could sleep on the dry hatch cover if you pulled away the chains."

The sailors grumbled something Noko could not hear. Rodrigo answered, "The hatch cover is too high for the captives to reach from below. But if you are afraid of a handful of women and children, then sleep wet all night."

Noko heard Rodrigo sing as he walked away. Then the chains began to rattle, as the sailors unhooked and dropped them to the deck. The two men settled themselves on the hatch cover.

Noko could scarcely breathe while he waited to be sure the guards were asleep. Had

Rodrigo talked loud and sang so that Noko would know the hatch cover was not chained down?

No, Noko decided. Rodrigo only thought the guards might as well be dry. Noko could never forget Rodrigo's pretended friendship the day he cut El Quibian's hair and came to eat in his house while all the time the Spaniards were planning to capture them. Now Noko hated the redheaded boy as much as he once had liked him.

Noko's anger did not keep him from taking advantage of the advice Rodrigo had given the sailors. Carefully he made ready. His brothers and sisters helped to steady his legs as Noko gave a sudden push under the hatch cover. The sleeping sailors, caught off guard, tumbled onto the deck. Before they realized what was happening in the darkness, Noko boosted the women and children through the opening.

Noko knew they were getting away. He could hear them running and the sound of splashes as their bodies hit the water. He was the last to swing himself on deck.

He heard startled cries from the guards. A heavy chain whipped across his back. It struck him on the head.

When Noko opened his eyes, he did not know how long he had been unconscious. He sat up and his head felt twice its size. He seemed to be alone in the dark hold. The ship was creaking and groaning. There was a grating sound and Noko knew the bottom of the ship was dragging on sand. They were crossing the bar, moving out of the river to the sea.

He knew when the ship anchored far offshore in the deeper currents of the ocean, for it pitched and rolled with the waves. Then he realized that there was water in the hold higher than his ankles. The ship was leaking.

The water had risen to his knees before sailors lifted the hatch, jumped down and began to man the pumps. One of them ordered Noko to help.

"Shipworms have bored tunnels through all the planking," a sailor said. "We are going to sea in a sieve."

"Still we are better off than the men left in the settlement to the cruel savages," another said.

The men pumped and bailed through the night. When other sailors came to take their places, Noko climbed on deck with the workers.

On the ship he saw a number of Indians who had joined Columbus on earlier stops he had made at the islands. Some of them had been hired as interpreters, but others had joined the voyage to see the wonderful things in Spain which the Spaniards had told them about.

Not me, Noko thought. I want to go home.

One of the Indians told Noko that the casks of drinking water had sprung leaks when the ship crossed the bar. Admiral Columbus had sent the ship's captain in the boat to get fresh

water upriver, and to bring news of the seventy men left in the settlement.

Noko, too, wanted to know what was going on ashore. Surely his father would attack the Spaniards now that the ships and their guns had left. Now that his family was free. He would think that Noko had drowned or had not yet made his way home.

Noko moved toward the rail to look at the shoreline in the distance, and came upon Rodrigo mending rope. Noko stared at him, then turned his back.

"When I cut your father's hair," Rodrigo said, "I didn't know what they planned to do."

For a moment Noko felt better. Then he remembered how easily the Spaniards' words had come when they asked to eat in his father's house and bent above El Quibian's wounded arm, pretending to heal him.

"You must not blame the Admiral," Rodrigo said to Noko's back. "If you knew the hardships he has suffered on his voyages, you would understand how important it is for him to make this settlement for Spain."

Noko spun around. "Not on the land of my people," he said

Rodrigo shrugged. "There is room enough and we have settled other places. This is the fourth voyage of Admiral Columbus. My father was with him on the first voyage ten years ago when he discovered the islands.

"My father said that Columbus didn't find this coast by chance. For years he believed there was land across the unknown ocean. He studied and planned and begged for ships and men to make the voyage to find it."

Noko acted as if he heard nothing, and Rodrigo again tried to explain.

"Columbus is an Italian but the rulers of his own nation did not believe him. He could get no help until he came to the King and Queen of Spain. In return he promised to claim land and gold for Spain.

"After Columbus proved that he was right, many men envied him. Some of his companions were disloyal and lied about him. He has endured shipwreck and mutiny. You can see that he is no longer young and shakes with malarial fever."

This was true, but Noko could feel no sympathy for him.

"Still," Rodrigo said, "the Admiral is the greatest navigator in the world. That's why so many of us chose to come with him. We are learning to be captains and pilots from a man who knows the sea better than anyone else. All our lives we will plant the flag of Spain wherever we go because of Columbus."

Noko turned. "I hope not one of you gets home," he said, and he walked away.

He was so tired that he lay on the deck and slept until a sailor shook him and ordered him to man the pumps below. When he climbed on deck again in the afternoon, he saw that the ship's landing boat had not returned from its trip ashore for water. Admiral Columbus was standing at the rail listening to the sound of cannon from the settlement.

"I must know how the fight is going," the Admiral cried, and climbed a mast to the highest part of the ship where he prayed aloud that he might see what was happening to his brother and the men and to the ship's boat with its captain and crew.

But he could see nothing, and for several days no one on the ships knew what was happening ashore. Among Columbus's three

ships, only one small boat remained. He dared not risk sending it ashore to be broken by the high waves on the river bar or by the Indians. Finally one of the young Spaniards volunteered to swim to shore if the boat would take him as close to land as the surf would allow.

The young man was gone all night, and when he returned Noko was among those who leaned over the rail to meet him. The Spaniard's face showed that his news was not good.

"When our boat went upriver for fresh water," he reported to the Admiral, "Indians waited behind trees at a narrow place and leaped upon our men and killed all of them. At the same time Indians attacked the settlement and killed or wounded many of our men. Captain Mendez moved the men to a cleared space on the riverbank and set up guns to keep the Indians at bay. But the men say they will not stay in this place. They beg you, Admiral Columbus, to take them all on board the ships again."

Columbus looked greatly troubled. He knew he should leave for La Española at once, for it was very dangerous to sail his worm-eaten ships during a season of windstorms. He looked at the waves which were still running so high over the bar that he could not rescue the men by boat.

Finally he said, "We cannot leave them. We must wait."

Columbus waited eight days while Diego Mendez directed the men at the settlement in making a raft from two dugouts joined together by timbers torn from the houses. With this raft the men were transported to the ships in two days. At last Columbus set sail for the island of La Española where he had built the settlement of Santo Domingo on an earlier voyage.

"We could never get home in these worm-eaten ships," Rodrigo said to Noko as they worked the pumps together. "But if we reach Santo Domingo, we will borrow better ships and sail for Spain."

Noko did not answer. He had to work beside these Spaniards, but he did not have to talk to them, or hope that they ever reached home.

He wished he knew that his family had reached the shore safely. His father and mother and sisters and brothers must be worrying about him, too. Now they would never know what had become of him.

For weeks Noko worked at the pumps

while men bailed day and night with kettles
and casks, but the water in the hold rose
to their waists, then to their shoulders. At
last one of the ships had to be abandoned
and its crew taken on board the remaining
two. With only one small landing boat, almost no food, with wind and sea currents running against them, Columbus commanded
his men to set the sails of their crippled
ships and head northward. Their one hope
was to reach La Española.

One morning Noko climbed from the hold
and fell on his back on the deck. He ached
in every bone and muscle. It seemed that he
had been on this rotting ship forever. His
stomach felt shrunk to the size of his thumb.
He had eaten nothing for days but a little
oil and vinegar on biscuit which crawled
with worms so that he had to close his eyes
to bite into it. Even Admiral Columbus had
nothing better to eat.

Suddenly Noko noticed that the sky overhead was filled with racing clouds, although the air on deck was close and hot. The ship rolled, riding a great swell.

Noko remembered. The sea had been like this the day he first sighted the sails of the strangers' ships and hurried to tell his father.

"Hurakan," Noko said now and sat up.

The bow of the ship rose to ride a great wave. But the hold was so full of water that the ship sank back. Water swept the deck from end to end.

Men leaped out of the hold like drowning rats and ran to take in sail so the ship could ride out the storm.

All day the ship pitched and trembled as the seas washed over her. Noko could not walk. He scrambled on his hands and knees when the ship leaned on her side.

Waves burst open cabin doors and ripped off ropes. Chests of blankets and clothing were swept overboard. Noko dodged a mast as it splintered and pitched into the waves, floated a moment, then sank.

"We're going over," men cried. But the ship righted herself again.

At night the storm seemed even more terrible. Noko had hoped the Spaniards would never reach home. Now he was as frightened as they were of the fire in the lightning, the howl of the wind, the thunder, and the mountainous waves.

In the darkness the two ships crashed together and Noko was thrown down a sloping deck. He dug into the planking with his fingernails, slipping and sliding until he caught against a timber. The two ships shuddered and creaked all night, rubbing against each other.

At daylight Noko saw Admiral Columbus inspecting the damage. Most of the masts and sails on both ships were gone. Only one anchor remained between them.

The Admiral turned to his men and said, "We must make for the island of Jamaica. Then if our ships can still be kept afloat, we will try to go on to La Española."

"We had better died in the storm," a sailor cried, "than starve to death on the sea as we'll do now."

Other men cried, "There's no settlement on Jamaica. We'll rot there. What have you brought us to!"

Columbus said nothing. Noko saw his lined face and weary eyes and was almost moved to sympathy. These sailors acted as if the Admiral were to blame for the storm. Then Noko remembered that all these men were his enemies. He would not feel sorry for the best of them.

Noko lost track of the days and nights they were on the sea, patching and bailing to keep the ships afloat. The water had almost reached the top of the hold when Columbus sighted the shore of Jamaica.

Somehow the men guided the half-sinking ships inside the reefs to a harbor which Columbus had visited on an earlier voyage. When the tide was highest, Columbus ordered the men to hoist all the sails and make for the shore. He ran the ships aground, side by side, close together so the men could leap from deck to deck.

At low tide, Columbus ordered the men to pile sandbags and timbers against the hulls so the ships could not be moved by the incoming tides.

"We will build cabins on deck and live here," he said to the assembled men. "And no man is to go on shore without permission. The Indians of Jamaica were friendly when we stopped here before, but if some among us are disobedient and roam about the countryside stirring them up, we do not know what they would do. We are marooned here and cannot risk trouble."

Angry cries came from the 116 men on the ships: "We are starving. We must go ashore and hunt food."

Captain Mendez quieted them. He volunteered to take three men and go to find an

Indian village and bring back food. He took with him the few things left to trade: a red cap, a pair of scissors, and some bells.

Noko stood at the rail and watched him leave. He longed to be off this worm-eaten ship. He would escape as soon as he could. But then, how could he ever reach home?

Rodrigo came and stood beside him and spoke as if he guessed what Noko was thinking. "It could be years before a ship will stop here or anyone know where we are marooned," he said. "But if we ever get home, Columbus will send you back to Veragua when a ship passes that way someday.

You have worked hard and Columbus is an honest and grateful man."

Noko believed nothing a Spaniard told him. He did not even glance at Rodrigo.

Noko had almost forgotten what fresh fruit and maize tasted like until Captain Mendez returned with food. He said that the Indians of Jamaica had been friendly and promised to visit the ships later with more food. As the days went by, the men grew stronger and talked of nothing but how to get home. Some of them demanded the right to roam the island and look for gold, but Columbus posted a heavy guard of trusted men. Even Noko could not pass them and was confined to the ships.

Admiral Columbus talked again and again with his brother and Captain Mendez and the other officers. At last the Admiral told the men that Captain Mendez had traded some trinkets for two Indian canoes, the kind made by hollowing out a large tree trunk. Some of the men must try to paddle them on the long and dangerous voyage to the island of La Española, and ask the Spanish governor of the settlement of Santo Domingo to send rescue ships to Jamaica.

"There is little hope that a ship will ever come here," Columbus said, "unless we go for help. Who will go?"

No one spoke. The men were miserable here but at least they were alive. Crossing more than a hundred miles of open sea in a clumsy Indian dugout was madness.

Captain Mendez stepped forward. "I will command one canoe," he said.

Another officer volunteered to command the other.

Rodrigo said to Noko, "I would rather die with a brave man like Diego Mendez than rot here." He stood beside the Captain.

Noko had to admit that he had never seen men of greater courage and daring than Captain Mendez and Admiral Columbus. But he remembered that the black-bearded Mendez had bent over his father's arm as if he wished to heal his wound, then seized him and captured his family. Noko would never willingly help him.

But when Mendez chose the men to go with him, Noko was one of them. He and Rodrigo were assigned to the Captain's canoe. Each crew was made up of six Spaniards and ten Jamaican Indians who had been hired to paddle.

"For the Indians are strong paddlers and swimmers," said Mendez. "They know how to right a capsized canoe and get back in it. We could not hope to make this voyage without their help."

Captain Mendez waited anxiously several days for the sea to become calm enough for a start. Then one morning they were ready. Noko entered the first canoe, carrying with him a gourd of water, cassava bread and fruit wrapped in palm leaves. The two canoes set off on the long voyage to La Española.

Noko soon realized that the calm they needed for the safety of the crossing meant

there was no breeze to cool them. The sun overhead felt like a bowl of red-hot coals baking and blistering them. When the sun finally sank below the water in the west, Noko's arms felt as if they would never stop aching.

But Captain Mendez urged the Indians and Spaniards to paddle all night. "We cannot risk a storm overtaking us," he said.

The morning of the second day the Captain told the paddlers to stop a few minutes and rest. Then he discovered that many of the Indians had drunk all the water from their gourds during the darkness. He dripped a few drops of water from his own small cask into their heat-blackened mouths, and they rowed again.

By the middle of the second day Noko's water was gone, too. He could scarcely hold up his head. When he grew faint, he went into the water, as the other Indians did, to refresh his body and rinse his mouth with salt water.

For two days and a night, he paddled against the strong ocean currents and saw nothing but water and sky. Then he heard Mendez say, "We should have reached a small reef island near La Española before this."

We must have lost our course, Noko thought. We're lost in an endless world of water which no one can drink. Well, he would get his wish. The Spaniards would never reach home. But neither would he.

The second night one of the Indians died of thirst. Several others grew so weak that they fell and lay in the bottom of the canoe. When the Spaniards took their turns at the paddles,

Captain Mendez rowed in the bow. Rodrigo paddled beside Noko.

The night was black and Noko could see nothing but sea fire shimmering underwater, burning green and blue and white in the waves.

Rodrigo said, "The light of the sea seems to follow us."

A bad omen, Noko thought, and he was afraid.

"Look," Captain Mendez cried.

A long way ahead of the canoes, a large pale moon came out of the water. At its base appeared a small hump of black as if a wave rode in front of the moon.

"An island," Captain Mendez shouted. He poured the last drops of water from his cask into the mouths of the paddlers. "We can reach it by morning," he encouraged the men.

At daylight they reached an island of bare reef and rock so small that they would not have seen it if the moon had not framed it.

There were no springs but the men ran from place to place to find rainwater which lay in hollows and crevices. They fell upon their stomachs and drank.

Captain Mendez shouted a warning, "Drink only a little. Our stomachs have shrunk." But he could not control them, and several Indians drank so much that they died.

Noko felt sick to his stomach and faint, but he managed to hunt shellfish along the shore with the other men. Captain Mendez took steel and flint from his pocket and made a fire. They cooked the shellfish and ate and rested until evening.

Then Captain Mendez said, "We must row tonight while the sun is down. La Española cannot be far now."

The captain of the second canoe, shaking with fever and exhaustion, said, "Can't we rest until morning?"

"See the clouds gathering, and the wind is rising," Mendez said. "We must not fail now, when we have endured so much. We will go on tonight."

Noko paddled all night, and at last heard surf breaking against reefs. At dawn he saw the coast of La Española. High waves dashed against its coral cliffs and narrow beaches. The rising sun made rainbows in their spray.

Ahead was the shore and safety, Noko thought, but it would not be easy to make a landing. The coast, as far as he could see, was a wall of sharp reef and heavy sea which the canoes must cross.

"Whether we live or die," Mendez said, "we go ashore here. Our canoes are too battered to attempt the trip around the island to the settlement. We can make the long walk across La Española to Santo Domingo, if we land here."

As the canoes neared the shore, a breaker caught them and rolled and tossed the men into the shallow water. Noko came up through a wave, blinking salt water from his eyes. He

saw his canoe sliding back to sea. He splashed
forward and gave it a strong push toward the
beach. One end swung around and struck him
on the head.

For a moment Noko knew nothing. Then
he found that Rodrigo had caught his shoul-
der and held his head above water. A giant
wave pulled Rodrigo under and Noko caught
him by the hair. The breaker lifted and
bounced them together upon the beach. They
fell forward upon the sand and, for a while,
were glad simply to breathe.

Finally Rodrigo said, "Admiral Columbus will not forget what you have done. He'll send you home when a ship goes to Veragua. I know he will."

For a moment Noko thought only of how much he wanted to see his father and family and home again. Then he turned his head to see Rodrigo. For the first time in many weeks, Noko really looked at the young Spaniard.

Rodrigo's skin was cracked and burned and blackened by the heat and salt spray, as Noko's was. Rodrigo's curly flaming-red hair was straightened and darkened by the salt water. To his surprise, Noko could see no difference between them now.

He looked down the beach and saw the other Spaniards and Indians sprawled on the sand. Light-skinned men and dark-skinned men looked exactly alike in their exhaustion. Together they had all endured hunger, thirst and pain, and almost lost their lives to find a way home.

Noko's heart was moved. There was no longer room in him for hate. He was thankful just to be alive. And for the first time since the Spaniards had captured him, Noko believed Rodrigo. He would go home again. And somehow he rejoiced that these Spaniards would reach home, too.